For Francis
and future campers everywhere
—F. L.

Henry Holt and Company, LLC, *Publishers since 1866*
115 West 18th Street, New York, New York 10011
www.henryholt.com

Henry Holt is a registered trademark of Henry Holt and Company, LLC
Compilation and illustrations copyright © 2003 by Frané Lessac. All rights reserved.
Distributed in Canada by H. B. Fenn and Company Ltd.

Library of Congress Cataloging-in-Publication Data
Camp Granada: sing-along camp songs / compiled and illustrated by Frané Lessac.
p.     cm.
Summary: Presents the lyrics for an assortment of popular camp songs, such as
"Rise and Shine," "Found a Peanut," "Do Your Ears Hang Low," "This Land Is Your Land,"
and "Kum Ba Yah." [1. Children's songs—Texts.  2. Songs.] I. Lessac, Frané, ill.
PZ8.3 .C1375 2003     782.42164'0268—dc21        2002007419
Every effort has been made to trace all the song creators, but if any have been
inadvertently overlooked, the publisher will be pleased to make the necessary
arrangement at the first opportunity.

Permission for the use of the following is gratefully acknowledged:
"Hello Muddah, Hello Fadduh," words and music by Allan Sherman and Lou Busch;
copyright © 1963 (Renewed) WB Music Corp. and Burning Bush Music. All rights
reserved. Used by permission. Warner Bros. Publications U.S. Inc., Miami, FL, 33014.
"This Land Is Your Land," words and music by Woody Guthrie; TRO,
copyright © 1956 (Renewed) 1958 (Renewed) 1970 (Renewed) Ludlow Music, Inc.,
New York, New York. Used by permission.

ISBN 0-8050-6683-7 / First Edition—2003 / Designed by Donna Mark
Printed in the United States of America on acid-free paper. ∞
10  9  8  7  6  5  4  3  2  1

The artist used gouache on Saunders Waterford paper to create
the illustrations for this book.

# Camp Granada

## Sing-Along Camp Songs

Compiled and illustrated by

### Frané Lessac

Henry Holt and Company · New York

# Contents

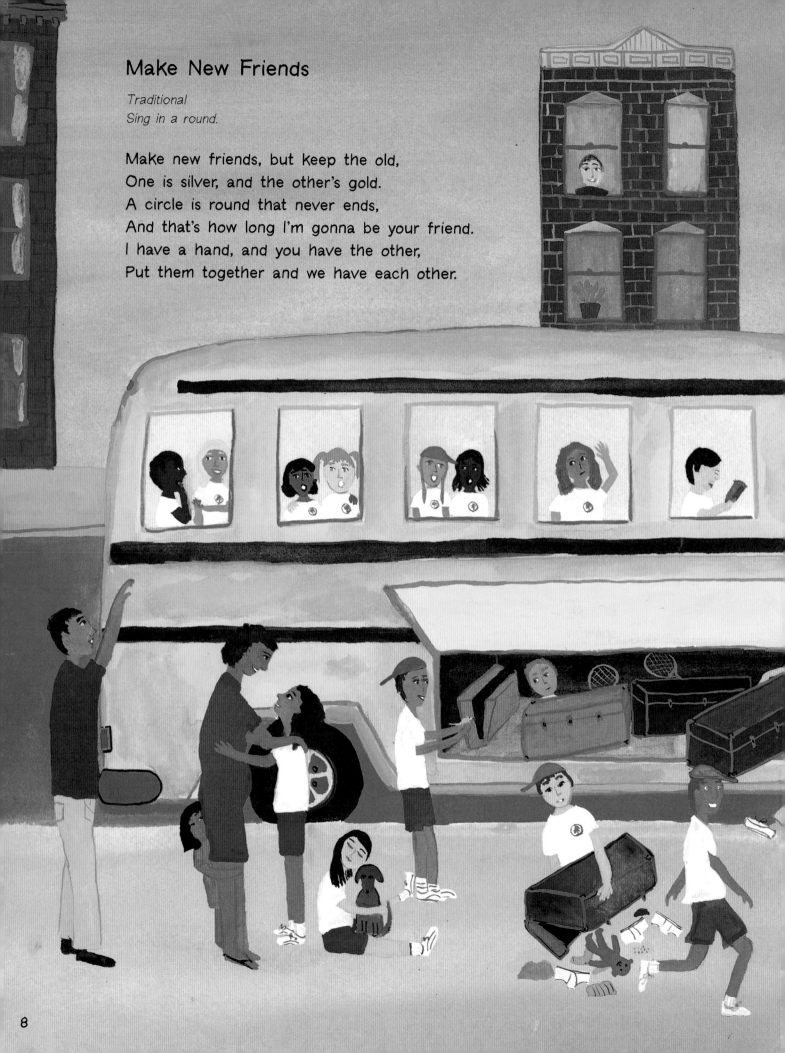

# Make New Friends

*Traditional*
*Sing in a round.*

Make new friends, but keep the old,
One is silver, and the other's gold.
A circle is round that never ends,
And that's how long I'm gonna be your friend.
I have a hand, and you have the other,
Put them together and we have each other.

9

# Rise and Shine

*Spiritual*

The Lord said to Noah, there's gonna be a floody, floody.
The Lord said to Noah, there's gonna be a floody, floody.
Get those animals out of the muddy, muddy.
Children of the Lord.

*(Chorus)*
Rise and shine and give God your glory, glory.
Rise and shine and give God your glory, glory.
Rise and shine and give God your glory, glory.
Children of the Lord.

So Noah, he built him, he built him an arky, arky.
So Noah, he built him, he built him an arky, arky.
Built it out of hickory barky, barky.
Children of the Lord.

*(Return to Chorus)*

The animals they came on, they came on by twosies, twosies.
The animals they came on, they came on by twosies, twosies.
Elephants and kangaroosies, roosies.
Children of the Lord.

*(Return to Chorus)*

It rained and poured for forty daysies, daysies.
It rained and poured for forty daysies, daysies.
Almost drove those animals crazy, crazy.
Children of the Lord.

*(Return to Chorus)*

The sun came out and dried up the landy, landy.
The sun came out and dried up the landy, landy.
Everything was fine and dandy, dandy.
Children of the Lord.

*(Return to Chorus)*

## Underwear

*Traditional*
*Sing to the tune of "Over There."*

Underwear, underwear, send a pair, send a pair I can wear.
For I left mine lying on a line a-drying,
And now I need them, they're not there.
Underwear, underwear, get a pair, get a pair, anywhere.
The bugle's blowing, I must be going,
For I've got to get there even if I have to go there bare.

# Pink Pajamas

*Traditional*
*Sing to the tune of "Battle Hymn of the Republic."*

Oh, I wear my pink pajamas in the summer when it's hot,
And I wear my flannel nighties in the winter when it's not,
And sometimes in the springtime and sometimes in the fall,
I jump right in between the sheets with nothing on at all.
Glory, glory, hallelujah!
Glory, glory, what's it to ya?
Balmy breezes blowin' through ya
With nothing on at all!

# Soap and Towel

*Traditional*
*Sing to the tune of "Row, Row, Row, Your Boat."*

Soap, soap, soap and towel; towel and water, please.
Merrily, merrily, merrily, merrily, wash your dirty knees.

# Do Your Ears Hang Low?

*Traditional*
*Sing to the tune of "Turkey in the Straw" and follow the actions for the first stanza.*
*Create your own for those stanzas that follow.*

Do your ears hang low?          (tug at earlobes)
Do they wobble to and fro?     (wave hands back and forth)
Can you tie them in a knot?     (tie an invisible knot)
Can you tie them in a bow?     (tie an invisible bow)
Can you throw them over your shoulder    (pretend to toss something over your shoulder)
Like a Continental soldier?    (salute)
Do your ears hang low?

Do your ears hang high?
Do they reach up to the sky?
Do they droop when they're wet?
Do they stiffen when they dry?
Can you semaphore your neighbor
With a minimum of labor?
Do your ears hang high?

Do your ears hang wide?
Do they flap from side to side?
Do they wave in the breeze,
From the slightest little sneeze?
Can you soar above the nation
With a feeling of elevation?
Do your ears hang wide?

Do your ears fall off
When you give a great big cough?
Do they lie there on the ground,
Or bounce up at every sound?
Can you stick them in your pocket
Just like Davy Crockett?
Do your ears fall off?

# Hail, Hail, the Gang's All Here!

*D. A. Esrom, 1917*

Hail, hail, the gang's all here,
Never mind the weather, here we are together;
Hail, hail, the gang's all here,
Sure we're glad that you're here, too!

Hail, hail, the gang's all here,
We're a bunch of live ones, not a single dead one;
Hail, hail, the gang's all here,
Sure I'm glad that I'm here, too!

# If You're Happy

*Traditional*
*Follow the actions.*

If you're happy and you know it,
Clap your hands.                              (clap, clap)
If you're happy and you know it,
Clap your hands.                              (clap, clap)
If you're happy and you know it
   and you really want to show it,
If you're happy and you know it,
Clap your hands.                              (clap, clap)

If you're happy and you know it,
Stamp your feet.                              (stamp, stamp)
If you're happy and you know it,
Shout "amen."                                 ("amen")
If you're happy and you know it
   and you really want to show it,
If you're happy and you know it,
Do all three.                       (clap, clap, stamp, stamp, "amen")

16

# Ship *Titanic*

*Traditional*
*Sing to the tune of "Little Old Cabin in the Lane."*

Oh, they built the ship *Titanic* to sail the ocean blue.
They thought they had a ship that the water wouldn't go through.
But the good Lord raised his hand,
He said the ship would never land.
It was sad when that great ship went down.

(Chorus)
Oh, it was sad, so sad.
It was sad, so sad.
It was sad when that great ship went down (to the bottom of the sea)—
Husbands and wives, little children lost their lives!
It was sad when that great ship went down.

So they built another ship called the *SS-'92*,
And they thought they had a ship that the water wouldn't go through.
But they christened it with beer,
And it sank right off the pier.
It was sad when that great ship went down (hit the bottom!).

(Return to Chorus)

The moral of this story is clearly plain to see—
Always wear a life preserver when you go out to sea.
For husbands and wives, little children lost their lives!—
It was sad when that great ship went down.

# A Sailor Went to Sea

*Traditional*
*Salute each time you sing "sea" or "see."*

A sailor went to sea, sea, sea.
To see what he could see, see, see.
But all that he could see, see, see
Was the bottom of the deep blue sea, sea, sea.

# Michael, Row the Boat

*Spiritual*
*Originated on the fishing boats of the Bahamas.*

*(Chorus)*

Michael, row the boat ashore, Alleluia!
Michael, row the boat ashore, Alleluia!

Sister, help to trim the sail, Alleluia!
Sister, help to trim the sail, Alleluia!

*(Return to Chorus)*

Jordan's river is chilly and cold, Alleluia!
Chills the body but not the soul, Alleluia!

*(Return to Chorus)*

The river is deep and the river is wide, Alleluia!
Milk and honey on the other side, Alleluia!

*(Return to Chorus)*

If you get there before I do, Alleluia!
Tell my people I'm coming too, Alleluia!

## Michael Finnegan

*Traditional*
*Repeat over and over again.*

There was an old man named Michael Finnegan.
He grew whiskers on his chinnigin.
The wind came around and blew them in again.
Poor old Michael Finnegan.
Begin again.

# John Jacob Jingleheimer Schmidt

*Traditional*
*Repeat song several times, each time softer and softer,*
*until the last verse when no sound is recited except*
*"Da, da, da, da, da, da, da," which is sung loudly.*

John Jacob Jingleheimer Schmidt,
His name is my name, too.
Whenever we go out, the people always shout,
There goes John Jacob Jingleheimer Schmidt!
Da, da, da, da, da, da, da.

BUDDY BOARD

24

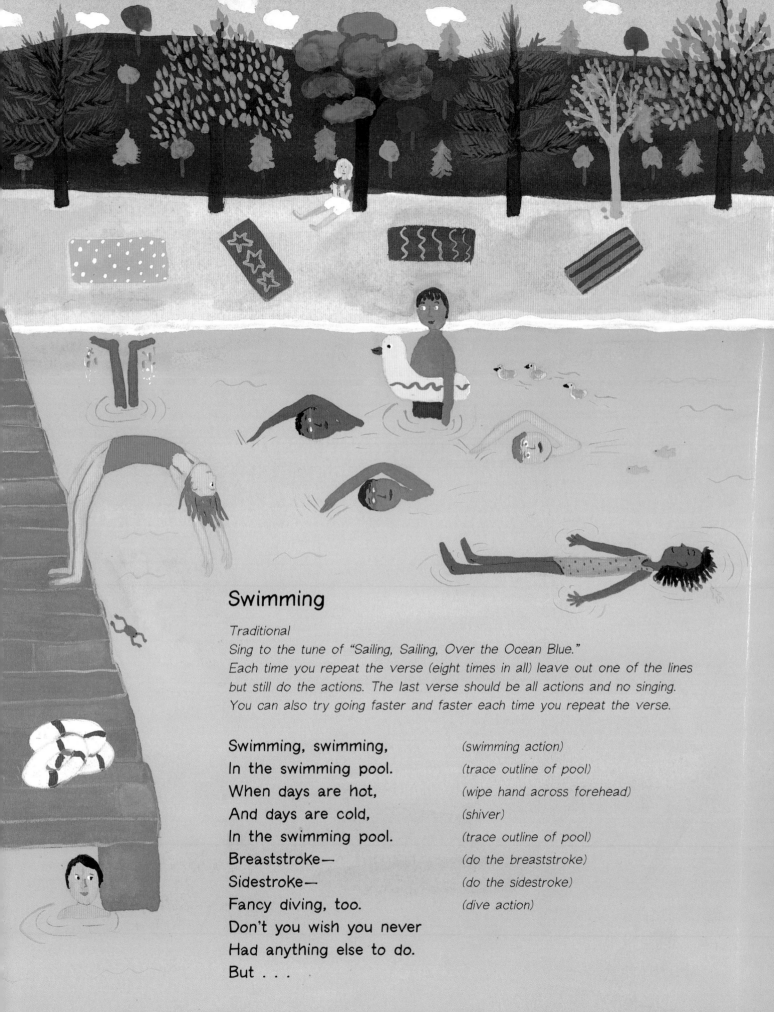

# Swimming

*Traditional*
*Sing to the tune of "Sailing, Sailing, Over the Ocean Blue."*
*Each time you repeat the verse (eight times in all) leave out one of the lines*
*but still do the actions. The last verse should be all actions and no singing.*
*You can also try going faster and faster each time you repeat the verse.*

| | |
|---|---|
| Swimming, swimming, | *(swimming action)* |
| In the swimming pool. | *(trace outline of pool)* |
| When days are hot, | *(wipe hand across forehead)* |
| And days are cold, | *(shiver)* |
| In the swimming pool. | *(trace outline of pool)* |
| Breaststroke— | *(do the breaststroke)* |
| Sidestroke— | *(do the sidestroke)* |
| Fancy diving, too. | *(dive action)* |
| Don't you wish you never | |
| Had anything else to do. | |
| But . . . | |

# Peanut Butter and Jelly

*Traditional*
*Follow the actions—Dig: pretend to dig. Smash: squish something between your hands.*
*Spread: use one hand to spread peanut butter and jelly over the other hand.*
*Pick: pretend to pick berries. The last time through the chorus, after eating the sandwich,*
*mumble the words as though there is peanut butter stuck to the roof of your mouth.*

*(Chorus)*
Peanut, peanut butter—jelly! Peanut, peanut butter—jelly!

First you take the peanuts and you dig 'em, and you dig 'em,
And you dig 'em, dig 'em, dig 'em.
And you smash 'em, smash 'em, smash 'em, smash 'em, smash 'em.
And you spread 'em, and you spread 'em,
And you spread 'em, spread 'em, spread 'em.

*(Return to Chorus)*

Next you take the berries and you pick 'em, and you pick 'em,
And you pick 'em, pick 'em, pick 'em.
And you smash 'em, smash 'em, smash 'em, smash 'em, smash 'em.
And you spread 'em, and you spread 'em,
And you spread 'em, spread 'em, spread 'em.

*(Return to Chorus)*

Then you take the sandwich and you bite it, and you bite it,
And you bite it, bite it, bite it.
And you chew it, and you chew it, and you chew it, chew it, chew it.
And you swallow, and you swallow,
And you swallow, swallow, swallow.

*(Return to Chorus)*

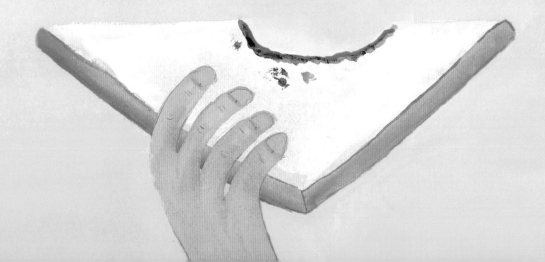

# Worms

*Traditional*

Nobody likes me.
Everybody hates me.
I think I'll go eat some worms.

*(Chorus)*
Big, fat, juicy ones; long, thin, slimy ones;
Itsy, bitsy, fuzzy, wuzzy WORMS!

First you get a bucket.
Then you get a shovel.
Oh how they wiggle and squirm!

*(Return to Chorus)*

First you bite the head off.
Then you suck the guts out.
Then you throw the skins away.

*(Return to Chorus)*

The first one was easy.
The second one made me queasy.
The third one got caught in my throat. UH! UH! UH!

*(Return to Chorus)*

Up comes the first one!
Up comes the second one!
The third one never made it down.

*(Return to Chorus)*

Everybody likes me.
Nobody hates me.
Why did I eat those worms?

*(Return to Chorus)*

# Bringing Home a Baby Bumblebee

*Traditional*
*Follow the actions.*

I'm bringing home a baby bumblebee,              *(hands are cupped together as if carrying a bee)*
Won't my mommy be so proud of me?               *(swing side to side)*
I'm bringing home a baby bumblebee—
Oooh, he stung me!                               *(make an "ouch" face)*

I'm squashing up my baby bumblebee,             *(hands are mashing together)*
Won't my mommy be so proud of me?               *(swing side to side)*
I'm squashing up my baby bumblebee—
Oooh, now it's all over my hands!               *(look at hands with "icky" face)*

I'm licking off my baby bumblebee,              *(pretend to lick your hands)*
Won't my mommy be so proud of me?               *(swing side to side)*
I'm licking off my baby bumblebee—
Oooh, that made me sick!                        *(hold stomach)*

I'm throwing up my baby bumblebee,              *(rock back and forth and hold stomach)*
Won't my mommy be so proud of me?               *(swing side to side)*
I'm throwing up my baby bumblebee—
Oooh, now the floor is all messy!               *(look at the floor in disbelief)*

I'm mopping up my baby bumblebee,               *(make believe you're mopping the floor)*
Won't my mommy be so proud of me?               *(swing side to side)*
I'm mopping up my baby bumblebee—
Oooh, he stung me again!                         *(make an "ouch" face)*

# Hello Muddah, Hello Fadduh (Camp Granada)

*by Allan Sherman and Lou Busch*

Hello Muddah, hello Fadduh,
Here I am at Camp Granada.
Camp is very entertaining,
And they say we'll have some fun if it stops raining.

I went hiking with Joe Spivy;
He developed poison ivy.
You remember Leonard Skinner;
He got ptomaine poisoning last night after dinner.

All the counselors hate the waiters,
And the lake has alligators,
And the head coach wants no sissies,
So he reads to us from something called *Ulysses*.

Now I don't want this to scare ya,
But my bunk mate has malaria.
You remember Jeffrey Hardy.
They're about to organize a searching party.

Take me home, oh Muddah, Fadduh,
Take me home, I hate Granada!
Don't leave me in the forest, where
I might get eaten by a bear.

Take me home, I promise I'll not make noise,
Or mess the house with other boys.
Oh, please don't make me stay,
I've been here already one whole day.

Dearest Fadduh, darling Muddah,
How's my precious little bruddah?
Let me come home if you miss me.
I will even let Aunt Bertha hug and kiss me.

Wait a minute, it stopped hailing,
Guys are swimming, gals are sailing.
Playing baseball, gee that's better,
Muddah, Fadduh, kindly disregard this letter!

ranada.
ining. And they
fun if it stops
hiking with Joe
ed poison ivy. You
nard Skinner. He got
oisoning last night after
the counselors hate the
And the lake has alligators,
he head coach wants no sissies,
he reads us from something
called

# Found a Peanut

*Traditional*
*Sing to the tune of "Clementine."*

Found a peanut, found a peanut, found a peanut last night.
Last night I found a peanut, found a peanut last night.

It was rotten, it was rotten, it was rotten last night.
Last night it was rotten, it was rotten last night.

Ate it anyway, ate it anyway, ate it anyway last night.
Last night I ate it anyway, ate it anyway last night.

Got a bellyache, got a bellyache, got a bellyache last night.
Last night I got a bellyache, got a bellyache last night.

Called the doctor, called the doctor, called the doctor last night.
Last night I called the doctor, called the doctor last night.

Operation, operation, operation last night.
Last night, operation, operation last night.

Died anyway, died anyway, died anyway last night.
Last night I died anyway, died anyway last night.

Went to heaven, went to heaven, went to heaven last night.
Last night I went to heaven, went to heaven last night.

Wouldn't take me, wouldn't take me, wouldn't take me last night.
Last night heaven wouldn't take me, wouldn't take me last night.

Was a dream, was a dream, was a dream last night.
Last night it was a dream, was a dream, last night.

Then I woke up, then I woke up, then I woke up last night.
Last night I woke up, I woke up last night.

Found a peanut, found a peanut, found a peanut last night.
Last night I found a peanut, found a peanut last night.

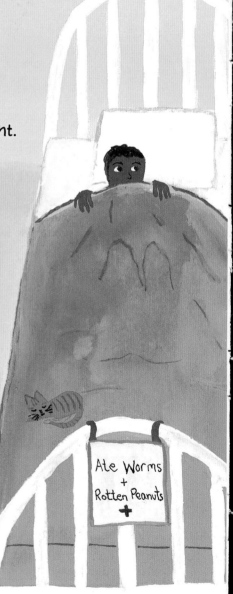

# In a Cabin in the Woods

*Traditional*
*Follow the actions. Repeat the song and leave out each of the lines one at a time,*
*but still gesture the actions. The last verse should be all actions and no singing.*

In a cabin in the woods,          (trace a cabin outline with your fingers)
Little man by the window stood,    (trace a window outline)
Saw a rabbit hopping by,           (two fingers of one hand like rabbit ears, hopping)
Knocking at his door—              (knock with hands)
"Help me! Help me! Help me!" he cried,  (throw arms up for each "help me")
"Or the hunter will shoot me dead!"     (aim a rifle)
"Come, little rabbit, come inside.       (stroke an imaginary rabbit in hands)
Happy we will be."                        (hug yourself)

# Little Bunny Foo Foo

*Traditional*
*Follow the actions.*

| | |
|---|---|
| Little Bunny Foo Foo | *(hold two fingers of one hand like* |
| Hopping through the forest, | *rabbit ears, hopping)* |
| Picking up the field mice, | *(scoop up an invisible mouse)* |
| And boppin' 'em on the head. | *(bop it on the head)* |
| Down came the good fairy | *(wave a magic wand)* |
|    and she said: | |
| "Little Bunny Foo Foo, | *(wag finger back and forth as if scolding)* |
| I don't want to see you | |
| Scooping up the field mice | *(scoop up an invisible mouse)* |
| And boppin' 'em on the head! | *(bop it on the head)* |
| I'll give you three chances, | *(hold up three fingers)* |
| And if you don't behave | |
| I'll turn you into a goon!" | *(make a funny face)* |

*(Repeat the song from the beginning, eliminating a "chance" each time.*
*When Foo Foo has used up his last chance, recite:)*

"I'm going to turn you into a goon." *Poof!*
And the moral of the story is: Hare today, goon tomorrow!

# This Land Is Your Land

*Woody Guthrie*

*(Chorus)*
This land is your land, this land is my land,
From California to the New York Island,
From the redwood forest to the Gulf Stream waters,
This land was made for you and me.

As I was walking that ribbon of highway,
I saw above me that endless skyway,
I saw below me that golden valley,
This land was made for you and me.

*(Return to Chorus)*

I've roamed and rambled, I followed my footsteps,
To the sparkling sands of her diamond deserts,
And all around me a voice was sounding,
This land was made for you and me.

*(Return to Chorus)*

# Kum Ba Yah

*Spiritual*

| | |
|---|---|
| Kum ba yah, my Lord, kum ba yah. | *(hand over hand, then arms out to either side)* |
| Kum ba yah, my Lord, kum ba yah. | |
| Kum ba yah, my Lord, kum ba yah. | |
| O Lord, kum ba yah. | *(extend arms upward)* |

*Other verses (repeat each line three times and
  end with "O Lord, kum ba yah"):*

| | |
|---|---|
| Someone's sleeping, Lord, kum ba yah. | *(sleeping pose)* |
| Someone's singing, Lord, kum ba yah. | *(cup hands around mouth)* |
| Someone's laughing, Lord, kum ba yah. | *(make a smile sign with your fingers)* |
| Someone's praying, Lord, kum ba yah. | *(make a praying sign)* |
| Kum ba yah, my Lord, kum ba yah. | *(hand over hand, then arms out to either side)* |

# Barges

*Traditional*
*It has been said that a young girl in a wheelchair wrote this song
as she watched barges from her hospital room window.*

Out of my window looking in the night,
I can see the barges' flickering light.
Silently flows the river to the sea,
As the barges too go silently.

*(Chorus)*
Barges, I would like to go with you,
I would like to sail the ocean blue.
Barges, have you treasure in your hold?
Do you fight with pirates brave and bold?

Out of my window looking in the night,
I can see the barges' flickering light.
Starboard shines green and port is glowing red,
I can see the barges far ahead.

*(Return to Chorus)*

How my heart longs to sail away with you,
As you sail across the ocean blue.
But I must stay beside my window clear,
As I watch you sail away from here.

*(Return to Chorus)*

# Tell Me Why

*Traditional*

Tell me why the stars do shine,
Tell me why the ivy twines,
Tell me why the ocean's blue,
And I will tell you just why I love you.

Because God made the stars to shine,
Because God made the ivy twine,
Because God made the ocean blue,
Because God made you, that's why I love you.

I really think that God above,
Created you for me to love,
He picked you out from all the rest,
Because He knew, dear, that I'd love you best.

*Silly Verses*

Tell me why the bugs do bite,
Tell me why the campfire won't light,
Tell me why the tent fell down,
Tell me why we slept on the ground.

Because they're hungry, the bugs do bite,
Because the wood's wet, the campfire won't light,
Because we're sloppy, the tent fell down,
Because we're crazy, we slept on the ground.

# By the Light of My Camp Flashlight

*Traditional*
*Sung to the tune of "By the Light of the Silvery Moon."*

By the light of my camp flashlight,
Wish I could see, what it was that just bit my knee.
Batteries, why did you fail me?
The chance is slim, the chance is slight,
I can last through the night, with my camp flashlight.

# All Night, All Day

Spiritual

All night, all day,
Angels watching over me, my Lord.
All night, all day,
Angels watching over me.
Now I lay me down to sleep.
Angels watching over me, my Lord.
Pray the Lord my soul to keep.
Angels watching over me.
If I die before I wake,
Angels watching over me, my Lord.
Pray the Lord my soul to take.
Angels watching over me.

42

## Taps

*Traditional*
*Taps was composed during the Civil War in 1862 by Brigadier General Daniel Butterfield. He created a unique bugle song for his brigade for the evening lights out. It became official army regulation and remains so to this day.*

Day is done, gone the sun,
From the lake, from the hills, from the sky;
All is well, safely rest, God is nigh.

Fading light, dims the sight,
And a star gems the sky, gleaming bright.
From afar, drawing nigh, falls the night.

Thanks and praise, for our days,
'Neath the sun, 'neath the stars, 'neath the sky;
As we go, this we know, God is nigh.

Sun has set, shadows come,
Time has fled, we must go to our beds,
Always true to the promise that we made.

While the light fades from sight,
And the stars gleaming rays softly send,
To thy hands we our souls, Lord, commend.

# He's Got the Whole World

*Spiritual*

He's got the whole world in his hands.     *[Repeat 4x]*

He's got the wind and the rain in his hands;     *[Repeat 3x]*
He's got the whole world in his hands.

He's got the sun and the moon in his hands;     *[Repeat 3x]*
He's got the whole world in his hands.

He's got the little bitty baby in his hands;     *[Repeat 3x]*
He's got the whole world in his hands.

He's got you and me, brother, in his hands;     *[Repeat 3x]*
He's got the whole world in his hands.

He's got everybody here in his hands;     *[Repeat 3x]*
He's got the whole world in his hands.

# Peace

*Traditional*

Peace, I ask of thee, O River,
Peace, peace, peace.
When I learn to live serenely,
Cares will cease.
From the hills I gather courage,
Vision of the day to be.
Strength to lead
And faith to follow,
All are given unto me.
Peace, I ask of thee, O River,
Peace, peace, peace.

# Dinah *From "I've Been Working on the Railroad"*

*Traditional, circa 1894*

Someone's in the kitchen with Dinah,
Someone's in the kitchen I know,
Someone's in the kitchen with Dinah,
Strumming on the old banjo.
Fee, fie, fid-ly-i-o
Fee, fie, fid-ly-i-o
Fee, fie, fid-ly-i-o
Strumming on the old banjo.

## Rock-a My Soul

*Spiritual*

Rock-a my soul in the bosom of Abraham,
Rock-a my soul in the bosom of Abraham,
Rock-a my soul in the bosom of Abraham,
Oh, rock-a my soul.

So high—can't get over it,
So low—can't get under it,
So wide—can't get around it,
Oh, rock-a my soul.

## Everywhere We Go

*Traditional*
*Repeat several times, louder each time until the last line, when you sing, "THEY MUST BE DEAF!"*

Everywhere we go,
People want to know
Who we are
And where we come from.
So we tell them
We're from [name of unit or camp],
Mighty, mighty [name of unit or camp],
And if they can't hear us,
We'll shout a little louder!

## Good Night Song

*Traditional*

Evening sunset paints the sky,
Smoke from campfire drifts on high,
Songs and stories we like best,
Just before we go to rest.

Good night to every camper, say good night,
To those away and these here in our sight,
The fun we've had we will not soon forget,
The things we've learned and the pals we've met.

And so, good night to every camper, say good night,
Above may each one's star send forth its light,
While songs and stories shared now wing their flight,
Good night, sweet dreams, good night!